KT-382-663

This Topsy and Tim book belongs to

Jennifer Slupek

This title was previously published as part of the _Topsy and Tim Learnabout_ series
Published by Ladybird Books Ltd
80 Strand London WC2R ORL
A Penguin Company

3 5 7 9 10 8 6 4

© Jean and Gareth Adamson MCMXCV

This edition MMIII
The moral rights of the author/illustrator have been asserted
LADYBIRD and the device of a ladybird are trademarks of Ladybird Books Ltd
All rights reserved. No part of this publication may be reproduced, stored in a retrieval system, or transmitted
in any form or by any means, electronic, mechanical, photocopying, recording or otherwise, without the prior consent of
the copyright owner.

Printed in Italy

At the Farm

Jean and **Gareth Adamson**

Topsy and Tim and Mummy were on
their way to Rosemary Farm. They
were going to see Mummy's friend
Mrs Stewart, the farmer's wife.

"May we help on the farm?"
asked Topsy.
Mrs Stewart gave them two
egg-boxes.
"Go along to the hen-house,"
she said, "and choose twelve
nice eggs from the hens' nests
to take home."

Some hens came to greet
Topsy and Tim and a duck
quacked cheerfully.
Topsy found some ducklings
learning to swim in an old bath.

A loud hissing noise startled Topsy and Tim. Four big, angry-looking geese were moving towards them. "We'd better run into the hen-house," said Tim.

The hen-house felt safe, but it was very gloomy. Soon their eyes grew used to the dark and they could see plenty of eggs in the hens' nests. Topsy chose six big eggs to fill her box. Four were white and two were brown.

The angry geese were on the path back to the farmhouse, so Topsy and Tim could not go that way.

They climbed the wall instead, being very careful with their eggs.
"Let's go back to the farmhouse this way," said Tim.

Topsy and Tim
were in the cows'
meadow. They did not know which way
to turn. Then they saw Farmer Stewart.
"I'm about to take these cows to the
milking-sheds," said Farmer Stewart.
"Will you give me a hand?"

Topsy and Tim helped Farmer
Stewart take the cows to the
milking-sheds, although the cows
knew the way themselves.
"Can we help milk the cows?"
asked Topsy and Tim.

"We will soon do that with our machines, thank you," said Farmer Stewart. "I've got a special job for you, though, if you'd care to help."

Farmer Stewart took a bucket of
new milk. He led Topsy and Tim to
a smaller shed.
There was a baby calf in the shed.
"Poor thing. It wants this milk," said
Farmer Stewart, "but it can't drink. It
only knows how to suck. Put your
eggs down somewhere and then
you can teach the calf how to drink
from the bucket."

Farmer Stewart showed Topsy what to do. She dipped her finger in the milk. Then she let the calf suck her milky finger.
The calf sucked so hard that Topsy felt nervous.

"Don't worry, it won't bite," said Farmer Stewart. Next, Topsy put her hand into the bucket. The calf went on sucking Topsy's finger until her hand and its nose were both in the warm milk. Then it was Tim's turn to feed the calf.

The calf soon discovered
how to drink from the
bucket without any help.
Topsy and Tim ran back
to the farmhouse to tell
Mummy all about it.

It was time for Topsy and Tim to go
home. As they walked down the lane
they heard a tractor behind them.
It was Farmer Stewart.

"Here are the eggs you forgot,"
he said, "and here is a big carton of
cream for your tea, because you were
so good and helpful at the farm."